Robin Hood

For Jeremy

Library of Congress Catalog Card Number: 95-80679
ISBN 0-8109-4428-6

Copyright © 1996 Margaret Early
First published in Australia in 1996 by Walter McVitty Books

Published in 1996 by Harry N. Abrams, Incorporated, New York
A Times Mirror Company
Printed and bound in Hong Kong

ROBIN HOOD

❀

Retold and illustrated
by
Margaret Early

❀

Harry N. Abrams, Inc., Publishers

HOW ROBIN HOOD BECAME AN OUTLAW

ONG, LONG AGO in England's Sherwood Forest, near the town of Nottingham, there lived a band of outlaws who were renowned for their wonderful skills with bow and arrow. Their leader was the greatest archer of them all, and his name was Robin Hood.

At that time, King Richard, known as Lionheart, was away on a Crusade in the Holy Land, while his brother, the greedy Prince John, ruled England in his place. Unlike Richard, Prince John cared little about his Saxon subjects. He ordered his Norman officials to tax them heavily and take away their belongings. The sheriff of Nottingham was the worst of these officials. Unable to pay the sheriff's high taxes, whole families died of starvation, and he put to death any hungry man he caught hunting for food in the king's forest. In desperation, honest people such as Robin Hood became outlaws.

Robin, whose real name was Robert, was the son of the Earl of Huntingdon, who had been killed while trying to stop the sheriff from unjustly seizing his land and possessions. After attempting to avenge his father's death, Robin fled to Sherwood Forest, taking with him his faithful servants, who chose to live as free men, even though outside the law, rather than as slaves under their Norman oppressors. Deep in the forest the outlaws built a secret hideout of log huts. They lived well, for there were caves to keep them warm and dry in winter, the forest abounded in wild game and its streams were full of fish. To blend in with their surroundings, they all wore clothes of Lincoln green, and whenever Robin blew on his silver horn three times his men would hurry to his side.

Soon the outlaws were joined by other brave and honest men, among them Nat the Weaver, Will Scarlett and Much the Miller's Son. 'If you wish to be part of our merry band,' Robin told all newcomers, 'you must agree to live by our rules, which are simple. We never harm the poor, the old, or any woman or child. We take only from the rich: we invite them to dine with us here in the greenwood, but they must pay for their meal. This money we give to the poor.'

Before long the rich and greedy lords and bishops dared not travel through Sherwood Forest without a small army for protection, for they knew that the price of Robin's food and drink would be high.

The outlaws had many well-wishers in the nearby villages and in the city of Nottingham. These friends could always be relied on to hide them from the sheriff's men and to share with them a simple meal of bread and soup, and give them fine goose feathers for their arrows. In return, the outlaws repaid their helpers with joints of venison from Sherwood Forest, or fat trout from its streams.

ROBIN HOOD MEETS LITTLE JOHN

ONE DAY while walking in Sherwood Forest Robin Hood came to a stream with a narrow wooden footbridge across it. Just as he was about to step onto this bridge a huge, bearded man suddenly emerged from the trees on the opposite bank. He had shoulders like an ox and carried a long, oak staff.

'Step back, good fellow, and allow me to cross first,' roared the stranger when he saw Robin.

'Step back yourself,' answered Robin. 'I stand aside for no man.'

'Is that so? Then let us settle the matter with our staves,' came the reply. 'If you are strong enough to knock me off this bridge and into the stream then you may cross first.'

Robin, who could never resist a challenge, quickly drew his sword, hacked and trimmed a branch from a nearby tree, and made himself a stout staff.

Then the two men stepped onto the narrow bridge and advanced towards each other. When they reached the middle the fight began. For a long time both men exchanged fierce and ringing blows with their staves, the one trying to dislodge the other from the narrow bridge. Robin, who was light and fleet of foot, tried every trick he knew, but his opponent, who was much stronger, parried every stroke. Finally, Robin received such a hefty clout that he tumbled headlong into the water.

Robin was always a good loser. 'You beat me, fairly and squarely,' he spluttered, as the stranger, laughing heartily, hauled him onto dry land. 'You are a mighty fighter, and no mistake. Pray, tell me, what is your name, and what brings you to Sherwood Forest?'

'My name is John Little and I come seeking Robin Hood,' was the reply. 'I hope to join his band of outlaws who live somewhere in these woods, for I am now an outlaw myself. I was caught poaching fish from a farmer's pond, but my captors were not strong enough to hold me. I cracked their heads together and made my way here, where I am told outlaws may live in safety, if they are honest men.'

'Then welcome to our merry company, John Little, for I am none other than the Robin Hood you seek.'

The two men laughed and clasped hands and swore to be friends for ever more.

'But we must change your name,' declared Robin. 'Henceforth you will be known as Little John, and you will be my right-hand man.'

And that is how Little John became a member of Robin Hood's band of outlaws in Sherwood Forest.

FRIAR TUCK JOINS THE OUTLAWS

T WAS WILL SCARLETT who told Robin about the mighty stranger who lived alone in a little cave by a stream in Sherwood Forest. This man looked far too well fed to be a hermit, Will said. Besides, he wore sandals and the rough, brown habit of a friar.

One day Robin decided to see this man of religion for himself. He set out for the stream, and soon came upon the stout friar. 'Hello, my fine fellow,' he called. 'Do you realise you are fishing in outlaw waters? By rights, everything you catch belongs to me and my men. However, I will allow you to fish here once a month, but only on condition that you agree to carry me across the stream on your back.'

'All in good time, my son, all in good time,' replied the friar, seizing his staff. This young scoundrel could have swum, he thought to himself, and the wetting would have done him good. He had not liked the way Robin had spoken to him. He caught only enough fish to eat and was not going to ask permission to do so from an outlaw.

'You look a strong man,' he said to Robin, ' but I doubt that you would be strong enough to carry *me* across the river on your back.'

As always, Robin was delighted to accept any challenge, and so he bent his back, lifted the enormous weight of the friar and somehow managed to lurch his way across the stream. 'There,' he gasped as he reached the opposite bank and set the friar down, 'you thought I could not do it. Well, now it is your turn to carry me.'

Back across the river they went, the friar carrying Robin as though he were but a small sack of flour. When they reached the middle, he gave a sudden jerk and flung Robin into the water. He roared heartily as he put his foot on Robin's chest and held him down. 'If I must ask your permission to fish in this stream, then must I now beg your permission to fish you out?' he asked, laughing.

'No, good friar,' spluttered Robin. 'You may fish from this stream whenever you like.'

The friar hauled him onto the bank. 'Then let us shake hands and part as friends,' he said. 'And may God go with you.'

'But why should we part?' asked Robin. 'Why not leave your cave and join me and my merry band in the heart of the forest? We are all good men and true, and could do with a priest, for we miss the word of God. My name is Robin Hood. Tell me, what is yours?'

'I am Michael Tuck, a simple friar, late of Fountains Abbey,' came the reply. 'I had a quarrel with my abbot, who has forgotten Christ's teachings in his desire to become rich. When I told him so, and reminded him of our vow of poverty, he wanted to punish me, but I escaped. I now lead a simple life, as our founder intended, here by this stream.'

'Then, good Friar Tuck, I invite you to join me and my company in Sherwood Forest.' So saying, he took Michael's huge hand and shook it and they swore to be friends for life.

CHRISTMAS AT GAMWELL HALL

HEN ROBIN HOOD was a boy his closest friends were Marion Fitzwater and her brother Mark. He taught them how to use bow and arrow, and to fight with such weapons as the quarterstaff and broadsword, at which Marian excelled, for she had strong wrists, was swift on her feet and was quite fearless.

Marian hoped to marry Robin one day, but when he became an outlaw her father forbade it, saying he did not want a bandit for a son-in-law. And so Marian was still pining for Robin when she arrived at Gamwell Hall where, every Christmas, Sir Guy Gamwell welcomed all his friends and neighbours to a grand feast. The great dining hall was filled with the wonderful smell of roasting pork and venison, while musicians played and the guests sang one Christmas carol after another.

When Sir Guy noticed an old man in the crowd singing in a wavering voice and roughly twanging a few strings on his harp, he called, 'I hope your appetite is better than your song, old greybeard, whoever you are.'

'That it is,' replied the man, suddenly throwing off his disguise of cloak and beard.

'Robin! It's Robin Hood!' cried Marian, running to him. They embraced and kissed each other under the mistletoe, while everyone laughed and clapped with delight.

'I journeyed to Gamwell Hall in disguise,' explained Robin, 'to make sure the sheriff's men would not recognise me along the way.'

Sir Guy welcomed Robin to his table and everyone sat down to eat.

During the feast a servant entered with a message for Sir Guy, who was pale and shaken when he stood to address his guests moments later. 'My friends,' he announced, 'it seems I am accused of high treason. There are rumours at Court that the sheriff is about to send his Norman rabble to arrest me.'

Robin Hood sprang to his feet. 'How could they think of doing such a thing to one of King Richard's most loyal subjects? Never fear, Sir Guy; your friends will come to your aid.' Turning to Marian he said, 'I do not know when we will meet again, but do not forget me, for I shall always be true to you.' After speaking privately to Sir Guy, he then left to return to Sherwood Forest.

At dawn the next morning the sheriff and his men rode up to Gamwell Hall expecting to take Sir Guy unawares, but were surprised to find that the drawbridge to the castle had been raised during the night. The sheriff's herald gave a blast on his trumpet and, in a loud voice, demanded the surrender of Sir Guy and all his possessions in the name of Prince John.

The reply was a mighty hail of arrows from Sir Guy's men, who had taken their places on the castle ramparts, and from Robin Hood and his outlaws, who suddenly appeared through the mists surrounding the forest. The terrified Normans turned and fled towards Nottingham.

SIR RICHARD OF THE LEA

ONE AUTUMN DAY Robin asked Little John and Much the Miller's Son to go to the Great North Road to find a wealthy passer-by to be his dinner guest. 'Bring me back an abbot or a bishop or a baron — someone who can pay generously for our hospitality,' he said.

And so the two men hid themselves beside the road, and before long a knight in tattered clothing came riding by. Little John stepped into view and hailed him. 'Welcome, good knight. My master, Robin Hood, wishes you to dine with him this day in Sherwood Forest.'

'If what I have heard about your master is true,' replied the knight, 'I would be honoured to be his guest, though today I have little appetite.'

The knight was duly entertained at a lavish dinner, at the end of which Robin said to him, 'Before you leave us, perhaps you would care to pay something towards the cost of this splendid meal.'

'That I would gladly do,' replied the melancholy knight, 'but it shames me to confess that I am unable to pay for my food, for I am now a poor man. Half a guinea is all I have.'

'If this be true,' declared Robin, 'I will not touch your money. In fact, if you are so much in need, I will even lend you some. But first, search his saddle bags, Little John, to make sure this gentle knight is telling the truth.'

Little John did as he was bid and, try as he might, he could find only half a guinea. Robin declared the knight to be an honest man and enquired how someone of his noble rank could have been reduced to such poverty.

'My name is Sir Richard of the Lea,' replied the knight, 'and I was a wealthy man until my son was taken prisoner while fighting at the side of good King Richard in the Holy Land. His captors demanded a ransom of one thousand pounds. I had only six hundred pounds, so to save his life I had to borrow the rest from the abbot of St Mary's. If this debt is not repaid in full by midday tomorrow my house and lands are forfeit to him.'

Friar Tuck frowned. 'You may as well expect comfort from a bed of nettles as mercy from the abbot of St Mary's. I know the rogue well,' he said.

'Little John,' ordered Robin, 'give Sir Richard four hundred pounds from our treasury, and some clothing worthy of a knight.'

This was no sooner said than done, and Sir Richard was overcome with gratitude as he embraced his new found friends. 'I must now leave you, but I give you my word that I will return exactly one year from today to repay in full my debt to you.'

So saying, he mounted his horse and started on his way.

THE ABBOT OF ST MARY'S

THE FOLLOWING DAY the abbot of St Mary's sat in stately splendour, surrounded by his monks.

'It will soon be midday,' he chuckled to himself, 'and when that moment arrives the fine house and all the lands which belong to Sir Richard of the Lea will be mine. I know that he will not have my four hundred pounds, for only last month Prince John sent his tax gatherers to demand money from him, and now he will have little or nothing to spare. Yet under our agreement his debt to me must be repaid in full this day, or he loses everything.'

At that moment Sir Richard entered the chamber. He presented a pitiful sight, with his old and tattered cloak wrapped around him. Humbly, he knelt before the abbot, his head held low. 'God's blessing, my lord abbot,' he said. 'I have come to beg your grace for more time to repay my debt, for I have not a penny of the money I owe you.'

'You have already had six months to pay,' sneered the abbot, 'and that is surely time enough. Leave this abbey at once, before I have you thrown out.'

Sir Richard was undaunted. 'What kind of servant of God is it who has no pity for a poor knight who kneels before him and begs for compassion?' he said.

Just then the midday bell began to ring.

'Enough!' shouted the abbot triumphantly. 'The appointed hour has come! From this moment onwards your grand house and all your lands are mine.'

'One moment, lord abbot. Do not be so hasty,' said Sir Richard, suddenly placing four leather bags, which he had kept hidden until now, before the astonished abbot. 'As you can see, I have found your money after all. Take your four hundred pounds!' And then he drew back his tattered cloak to reveal the fine garments in which he was now dressed. 'I am no false knight, but you are a villain and a thief who hides beneath the cloak of religion.'

Sir Richard turned and walked away, leaving the abbot speechless, the colour drained from his face.

MARIAN MEETS ROBIN IN THE FOREST

HREE YEARS after Robin Hood became an outlaw, Marian learned that her father was planning to marry her off to Sir Guy of Gisborne, a widower almost twice her age. Horrified at the thought of marrying someone she did not love, she decided to run away and join her friend Robin. Helped by her brother Mark, she disguised herself as a knight and, armed with a sword, set off for Sherwood Forest.

Now it happened that on that same day Robin had business in Nottingham and had gone disguised as a beggar. As he was walking home through the forest he saw a young knight approaching on horseback, and for a moment it crossed his mind that he had seen this young fellow somewhere before.

'What is your business here in the forest?' he challenged, drawing his sword.

'What is *my* business here? you ask. What is yours, beggar-man?'

Neither recognised the other.

'If I were you I would go back the way you came, and quickly, before there is trouble,' Robin said, 'for you are now in outlaw country, and outlaws do not take too kindly to strangers trespassing on their land.'

'I will not be turned back by the likes of you,' said Marian, drawing her sword. 'Come, let us fight it out, and may the better man win.'

And so the fight began. Robin was a fine swords-man, but Marian was an equal match for him, so nimble and skilful was she. Time and again she caught him off-balance, and time and again she was able to turn his blade aside. When finally she forced him backwards, Robin's foot caught in a tree root and he fell helplessly to the ground as his sword flew through the air.

'Now, my good man,' said Marian, her sword at his throat, 'get up and walk. I want to meet this outlaw band and see for myself where you hide yourselves in the forest. But most of all I want to meet your leader, Robin Hood, for I have come to Sherwood Forest to marry him.'

At this she removed her helmet. Robin gasped as he saw Marian's hair fall tumbling over her shoulders. With a cry he pulled off his false beard and the two lovers, recognising each other for the first time, fell into each other's arms.

That night there was much rejoicing in the forest and a few days later Robin and Marian became husband and wife. There were two weddings, the first in the little chapel which had been built for Friar Tuck in the greenwood, the second in a nearby village church, with Will Scarlett and twenty archers keeping guard outside.

That is how Maid Marian came to Sherwood Forest, and the outlaws never tired of hearing how she had fought their leader sword to sword, and finally forced him to yield.

ALAN a'DALE

ROBIN AND MARIAN were walking through the forest one day when suddenly they came upon a young man who was playing a harp and singing a sad little song:

'*Alack, alack and well-a-day,*
My love is lost forever,
And I shall hold her in my arms,
Ah, never, never, never.'

Tears rolled down his cheeks as he sang the last, heartfelt line.

'Young man,' said Marian, 'please tell us who you are, and what has made you so unhappy.'

'My name is Alan of Barnsdale,' was the reply, 'but people call me Alan a'Dale. I love a girl named Alice, but tomorrow she is to be married by the bishop himself to a rich old baron at Papplewick church. I know Alice loves me dearly, but her father wants his daughter to be married to a rich man, not a poor minstrel.' As he began his sorrowful song once more the tears flowed anew, and Robin decided then and there to help Alan a'Dale get his sweetheart back.

Early next morning he sent his finest archers to Papplewick: some hid in the upstairs gallery while others waited in the bushes outside the church. When the time came, Robin Hood, Friar Tuck and Alan a'Dale joined the congregation and went into the church, dressed as simple peasants.

Soon the bishop entered, followed by the bridegroom — a wizened, stooped old man with a little grey beard.

Then the unhappy Alice arrived, leaning on her father's arm. Her face was pale and her lips were trembling.

When the bishop began the wedding service Robin Hood suddenly stepped forward. 'My lord bishop,' he said loudly, 'a crabbed old man has no business marrying this beautiful maiden. Winter should never be wed with spring.'

'How dare you interrupt!' gasped the bishop. 'Get back to your place at once.'

But Robin continued. 'If there is no true love between a man and woman then it is a sin against God for them to marry.'

'Guards! Arrest this impudent fellow!' shouted the enraged bishop.

'If your men move they will die,' came a voice from the gallery above. 'And so will you, bishop.' It was Will Scarlett. By his side stood ten archers with bows bent and arrows ready.

Then Robin said to Alice, 'Young woman, is there anyone here, other than this ancient fellow, whom you would rather marry?'

When Alice turned round and saw her beloved Alan a'Dale she flew to his tender embrace. And so they were married that very day in the church, not by the bishop, who had fled for his life, but by Friar Tuck. Then the happy couple left with Robin and Marian for Sherwood Forest, where a wedding feast was prepared, and by the time the bishop returned with the sheriff and one hundred archers Papplewick church was empty and the door was locked.

THE TWO MONKS

ONE DAY Little John, Will Scarlett and Much the Miller's Son were at the Great North Road waiting for a suitable dinner guest, when along came two monks dressed in grey robes, followed by their servants. Little John sprang out in front of the leading monk. 'Stay where you are,' he said, aiming an arrow at his heart. 'In the name of my master, Robin Hood, you are to join us for dinner in the greenwood. If you refuse I will let this arrow fly.'

When the servants heard the name Robin Hood they turned and fled. Much and Will then led the monks' horses by their bridles and when they arrived at the camp Robin greeted them courteously.

The first monk protested: 'This is an outrage! I am the chief steward at St Mary's Abbey, and this is my clerk. We travel to London on important business for the Church.'

'If, indeed, you are from St Mary's Abbey then you are doubly welcome here,' Robin replied. 'Pray be seated at our table. You may be sure you will be well fed.'

The two monks sat and ate, somewhat nervously, and when the meal was over and they had drunk the last of their wine Robin said to them, 'It is the custom for our guests to pay for the food they eat, each according to his means. How much money do you carry with you?'

The chief steward waited a long moment before replying , 'We have but twenty shillings for the whole of our journey.'

'If that is all you have,' replied Robin, 'I will give you as much again to help you on your way. But first we must be sure that you are telling the truth.'

The two monks grew pale with fear and began muttering prayers as they watched Little John approach their saddle bags and begin searching.

'Let's see what we have here,' he said, bringing a rather heavy bag to the table. He emptied out its contents and began counting as the two monks looked helplessly on. 'Eight hundred pounds!' he declared at last.

'But this money is not ours,' spluttered the chief steward. 'It belongs to Prince John. It is money the Church owes him.'

'Prince John is a traitor to his brother, King Richard, and to his subjects,' replied Robin. 'There are many good, honest folk more deserving of this money than Prince John. Go back at once to St Mary's Abbey, give the abbot my greetings and thank him for his kind donation.'

Threatening to have their revenge on Robin Hood, the two monks were escorted through the forest and sent on their way to retrace their steps to York, and St Mary's Abbey.

SIR RICHARD REPAYS HIS DEBT

OON AFTER the two disgruntled monks departed, Sir Richard of the Lea came riding into Robin's camp, followed by his men.

'Greetings, Sir Richard,' called Robin. 'When I saw the leaves on the trees turn golden I knew it would not be long before we had the pleasure of your company.'

'And greetings to you, Robin Hood,' replied the knight. 'It is, indeed, a twelvemonth since last we met.'

Sir Richard was then introduced to Marian, Alice and Alan a'Dale and others who had joined the outlaw band in the previous year.

'Good friends,' he continued, 'as promised, I have returned to Sherwood Forest to settle my debt to you. I have lived carefully this past year and am now able to repay your four hundred pounds and, for good measure, a further twenty pounds in interest.'

'Thank you, Sir Richard, but you may keep your money, for your debt has already been repaid,' replied Robin. 'And by none other than the abbot of St Mary's himself! It is scarcely one hour since two of his monks left us a donation of double the amount of money you borrowed from us just one year ago.'

Robin then told the knight what had happened that day and they laughed heartily together over the tale. Then Sir Richard urged Robin to take the money he owed him, but Robin refused. He suggested instead that the knight use it to buy more horses and armour for his own protection, for his life would now be in danger: the abbot of St Mary's and Prince John were sure to accuse him of being in league with the outlaw, Robin Hood.

That evening there was a grand feast in Sherwood Forest and each of Robin's men was presented with a new bow of the finest yew and a dozen arrows apiece, with shining silver points and peacock feathers.

In the weeks that followed, Robin made careful enquiries of the people who lived in the villages near Sherwood Forest. Wherever he found poverty, need and hardship, he distributed the eight hundred pounds he had taken from the two monks.

In that bitter winter many humble people had cause to bless the name of Robin Hood and his loyal followers.

THE SILVER ARROW

AS ROBIN HOOD'S exploits became more and more daring, the sheriff of Nottingham decided it was time to put a stop to his enemy. He would have his revenge on this bold outlaw once and for all. Knowing that the men of Sherwood Forest were proud bowmen, every one, he arranged to hold an archery contest, open to all comers. The prize for the winner would be a silver arrow. He felt certain that such a contest could not fail to lure Robin Hood and his men to Nottingham to display their skills. The sheriff's own men would be armed and waiting and, on a given signal, would arrest every man dressed in Lincoln green.

And so the sheriff sent messengers around the country to spread word of the great competition, and he made doubly sure that the news reached Sherwood Forest.

On the appointed day Robin said to his friends, 'Let us go to Nottingham to bring back the sheriff's prize.'

But Marian begged him not to go. 'It is a trap, and you will be killed,' she pleaded.

'Do not worry, my love,' Robin replied. 'Nobody there will recognise us. We will leave off wearing our familiar Lincoln green and go dressed as humble country folk instead.'

In Nottingham that day there was much ado in the castle square: children danced, and there were jugglers, tumblers and musicians, and even a performing bear to entertain the crowd. Many were the games and tests of skill, but the most important of all was the archery contest. Lords and ladies joined the sheriff to watch from a raised stand which gave them a perfect view of some wonderful feats of marksmanship. Many fine archers had come from far and wide, but none could match a man in a red cloak whose arrows hit the middle of the target three times in a row.

The final test of skill came when the large, circular target was replaced by a slender wand from a willow tree. With three tries each, no archer was able to hit this stick, but the stranger in the red cloak split it in half at his first try. When he repeated this performance, not just twice but three times, there were wild cheers from the crowd. But there were none from the sheriff, who was now certain that his plan had worked. The stranger must be the man he sought, for none but Robin Hood could perform such a feat.

'Guards!' he shouted. 'Seize this man at once! He is our enemy Robin Hood, the common outlaw and traitor. I have him at last!'

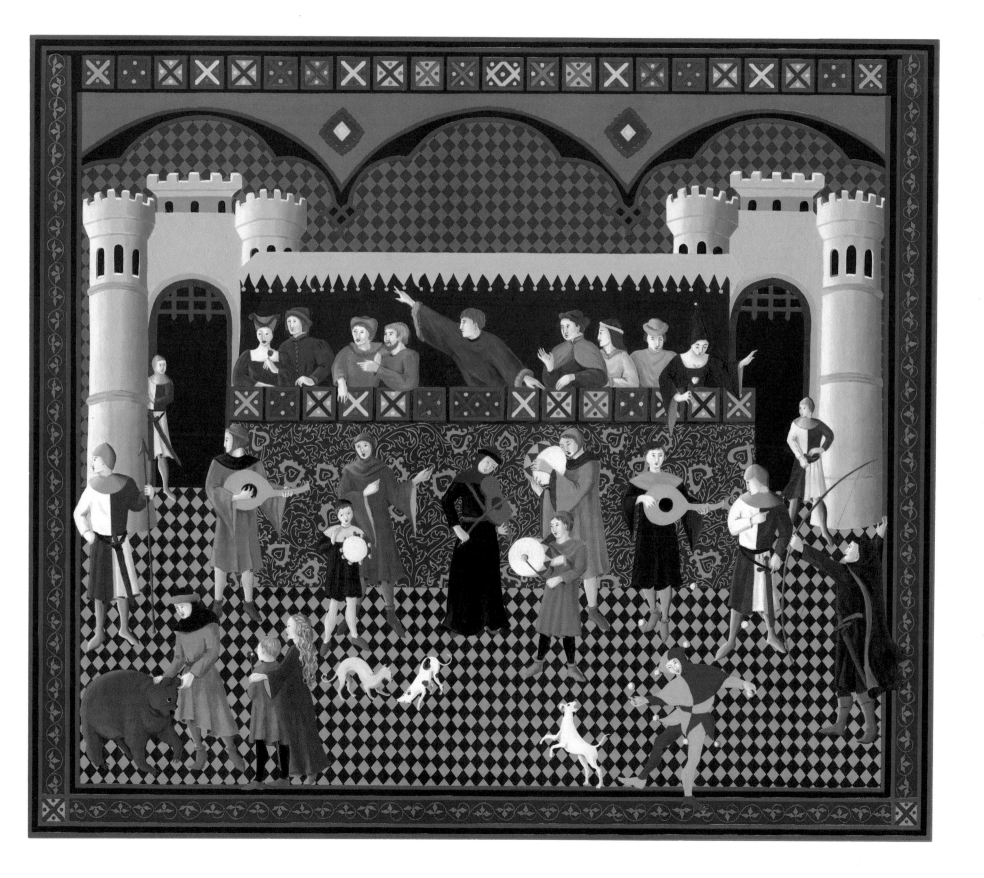

THE ESCAPE FROM NOTTINGHAM

HE SCENE which followed was one of great confusion, as Robin's men moved forward to confront the sheriff's guards. In the battle, arrows flew, swords clashed, people screamed and innocent children were trampled under foot. As the outlaws were not dressed in Lincoln green, the sheriff's men could not easily identify them and so lashed out at anyone in their way. Many helpless bystanders were injured or killed.

The outlaws fought bravely, but when he saw that they were hopelessly outnumbered Robin gave them the order to retreat.

In his escape from the castle Little John was hit in the leg with an arrow. 'Robin, good friend,' he cried, 'I cannot go on. Please take my sword and slay me at once, before the sheriff's men take me alive.'

'Not for all the gold in Christendom would I do so,' said Robin. 'I would rather die at your side than leave you here alone.'

Robin and Much carried Little John to shelter and made a crude stretcher for him, while the outlaws gave them protection. They fired their arrows with such precision that many of the sheriff's men turned and fled for their lives rather than risk death.

Meanwhile, Sir Richard of the Lea had been watching the battle from his castle and when he saw the outlaws coming his way he ordered the drawbridge to be lowered. He was at the gateway to meet them when they arrived. 'Quickly, my friends, come all of you inside my hall, where you will be safe,' he said.

Little John was carried in first, and the others followed. Sir Richard's men then raised the drawbridge and took up their positions on the castle ramparts.

When the sheriff arrived at the castle he shouted, 'In the name of Prince John, I command you to release his enemies into my custody.' But when he saw how many soldiers Sir Richard had, all with arrows pointed straight at him, he gave up his demands and returned to Nottingham a defeated man.

Robin thanked Sir Richard for his help, and after a great celebration the outlaws returned to Sherwood Forest later that night under cover of darkness. Little John remained behind in the care of Sir Richard's wife, who treated his wound so well that his leg soon mended and in no time he was able to rejoin his friends in the greenwood.

THE STRANGER IN THE FOREST

ONE EVENING as he was out hunting, Robin Hood saw, riding towards him, a knight who wore the cross of a crusader on his breast.

As he drew near, the knight called a greeting. 'Good evening, my fine fellow. Although I am unfamiliar with these parts, I am surprised to find anyone abroad in this forest at an hour when most honest men are in their beds.'

Robin laughed. 'Then neither of us is an honest man, so let us shake hands as a pair of rogues. Permit me to bid you welcome to Sherwood Forest.'

'This forest must surely belong to the king, yet you speak as though it were yours. Perhaps it is, but I have been away on a pilgrimage in foreign lands these past years and know not what has been happening in this country.'

Robin then told the stranger of the dreadful state of England under the misrule of Prince John and his greedy barons, in the absence of King Richard. He told of Norman wrongdoing and the suffering of many honest Saxon families. He explained how he, once Robert, heir of the murdered Earl of Huntingdon, had been forced to become Robin Hood, the outlaw, and told of his many clashes with the evil sheriff of Nottingham.

'Good pilgrim,' Robin said at last, 'if you would care to join us, you may dine on King Richard's venison this very evening. Will you be our guest?'

'I will gladly accept your kind offer,' said the stranger, 'for I am as hungry as if I had walked all the way from Jerusalem, and as thirsty, too.'

That evening the knight was well entertained in Sherwood Forest. He was seated beside Marian, and was much taken with her beauty, wit and grace.

At the end of the meal Robin proposed a toast. 'Let us drink to our good King Richard, far away in the Holy Land. May he soon be returned to his country and to his suffering people.'

'To King Richard and his return!' cried everyone present.

When the toast was completed the stranger rose to his feet. In a proud and noble voice he announced: 'My friends, I can keep the truth from you no longer. I am no knight, but your king, Richard, known as Lionheart, newly returned to England.'

There was a moment of stunned silence before the outlaws recovered from their surprise to give a great cheer. 'Long live King Richard!'

Robin and his men then bared their heads and fell to their knees.

'Arise, Lord Huntingdon,' said the king. 'Your lands and titles I hereby restore to you, from this moment onwards.'

King Richard spent that night in Sherwood Forest, sleeping under a cloak of Lincoln green. The following morning he rode into Nottingham, with Robin and his men forming a guard of honour.

When the sheriff saw them approaching he fled for his life, and was never seen in Nottingham again.

THE DEATH OF ROBIN HOOD

O ENDED the great days and deeds of Sherwood Forest. After King Richard's return, Robin Hood reclaimed his family home, Huntingdon Lodge and its estate, and with Marian at his side, and surrounded by old friends, he lived on for many happy years.

One day in his eightieth year Robin fell sick with a fever. He was so ill he could scarcely stand.

'We must get him to Kirklees Priory,' said Friar Tuck. 'The prioress there is renowned for her skill in curing illnesses.'

When Robin, Marian and Little John arrived at Kirklees they were welcomed by the prioress, who quickly discovered that her new patient was once the notorious outlaw, Robin Hood. She showed him to his room and sent Marian and Little John to the dormitory, telling them not to disturb her patient until the following day.

For here had befallen a terrible chance. The prioress knew of the two monks who had been robbed of eight hundred pounds in Sherwood Forest many years earlier, for one of those monks was her brother. She had sworn at the time to avenge his humiliation if ever the opportunity arose, and now, after all these years, fate had finally delivered her brother's enemy into her hands.

She put Robin to bed and opened a vein in his arm to let the blood run free, which was a common practice in those days. Tired from the fever and the journey, Robin fell into a deep sleep.

Some time later, when he awoke and saw his arm, he knew he was bleeding to death. Summoning what little strength he had, he raised his silver horn to his lips and blew on it three times.

Marian and Little John heard Robin's call and rushed to his side. They were shocked by what they saw: Robin was only just alive, and his blood had stained the bed a deep red.

'A thousand curses on this wicked prioress,' cried Little John. 'She has destroyed the noblest man in England. I will kill her for this terrible deed, and burn Kirklees to the ground.'

'No,' said Robin feebly. 'I have never hurt a woman in my life; nor will I at its end. Help me to the window. Dearest Marian, pass me my bow. I will shoot one more arrow before I die. Bury me wherever it falls, Little John, and tell no man the place.'

And so, for the last time, and with great effort, Robin drew his bow. A moment later the lone arrow soared over the walls of the abbey and into the forest beyond.

Robin died soon afterwards in the arms of the two people he had loved most in all the world. Little John sobbed bitterly while Marian closed Robin's eyes and wept for her dead lord.

But although Robin Hood died, his spirit lived on, and does so to this day, in the hearts of all people who believe that freedom is more precious than life itself, and that evil must never be allowed to triumph over what is right and good.

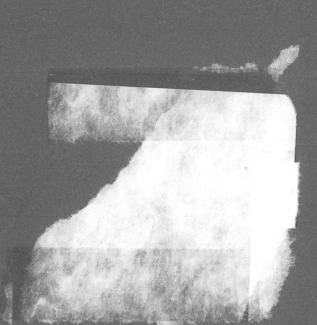